Stay away from the junkyard!

Reading Level: 3.9
Point Value: 0.5

ACCELERATED READER

W9-BJL-379

Stay Away from the Junkyard!

Tricia Tusa

Aladdin Paperbacks

First Aladdin Paperbacks edition 1992

Copyright © 1988 by Tricia Tusa

Aladdin Paperbacks
An imprint of Simon & Schuster Children's Publishing Division
1230 Avenue of the Americas
New York, NY 10020

Printed and bound in Hong Kong by South China Printing Company (1988) Ltd.
10   9   8   7   6   5   4   3
The text of this book is set in 14 pt. Egyptian 505 Light.
The illustrations are rendered in pencil and watercolor.

Library of Congress Cataloging-in-Publication Data
Tusa, Tricia.
   Stay away from the junkyard! / Tricia Tusa. — 1st Aladdin Books ed.
       p.   cm.
   Summary: Despite what the people of Jasper, Texas, think, Theodora feels
Old Man Crampton, his pet pig, and his junkyard are just dandy.
   ISBN 0-689-71626-5
   [1. Friendship—Fiction.]   I. Title.
PZ7.T8825St   1992
[E]—dc20   91-38498

For all the
Old Man Cramptons
of the world

Theodora was arriving in the small town of Jasper, Texas, for her first summer at Aunt Mazel's.

The train dropped her off right in front of her aunt's house.

Aunt Mazel's housekeeper, Mrs. Percy, greeted Theo. "I expect you'll keep your room tidy and wipe your feet before entering the house. And by all means stay away from the junkyard! That odd-looking Old Man Crampton lives there with a pig he calls Clarissa. He's clearly mad."

"Now, now," said Aunt Mazel, "he's still a newcomer. Nobody really knows him."

"And nobody's going to," muttered Mrs. Percy as she left the room.

The next morning, Theo set out for the vast, un-
explored land beyond, sure she'd discover a couple of
Indian hideouts, at least one Spanish treasure, and
maybe even a cow or two.

Her first stop was Mudd Doogan's General Store for a root beer. "How about that!" said Mudd Doogan. "So you're Miss Mazel's niece! You have yourself a good time here in our proud town. Only stay away from the junkyard! The rumor is, Old Man Crampton has no teeth, so he swallows kids whole."

Lured into Miss Betty Anne's bakery by the delicious aroma, Theo bought an oatmeal cookie. "Mind you," Miss Betty Anne warned, "don't set foot near that old junkyard. I hear the place is booby-trapped with holes so deep you could fall all the way to China."

After playing awhile with the kids in town, Theo
decided to go off on her own. She headed north toward
a nearby hill.

Over the hill Theo came to a stumbling halt. Before her was the most breathtaking sight.

A mountain of glistening objects towered above her, objects of every shape and size and color, one on top of another. She gasped! "Maybe this is the Spanish treasure!"

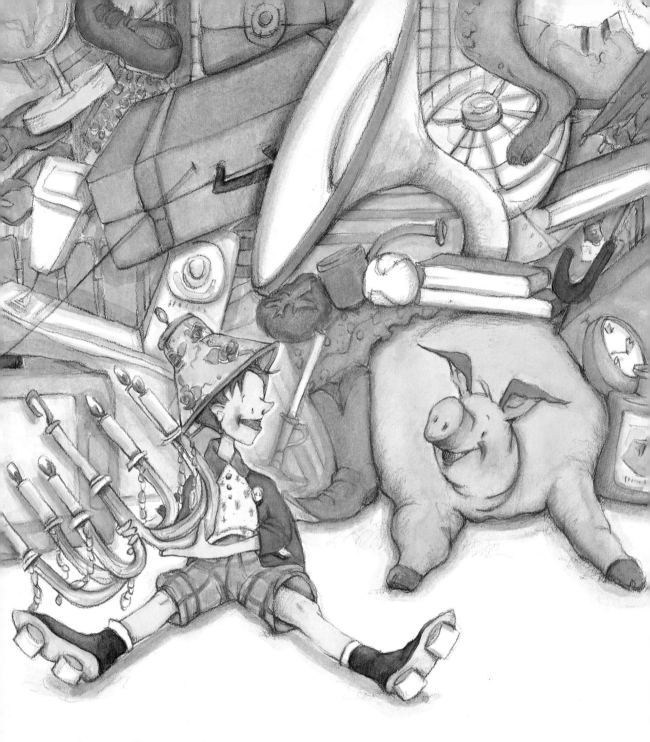

Rummaging through, Theo found an old trumpet,
a lampshade, a chandelier. She squealed with delight.
Suddenly the pile began to move. Theo squealed
even louder, as out crawled the plumpest pig ever.
"Oink!" announced the pig.

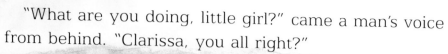

"What are you doing, little girl?" came a man's voice from behind. "Clarissa, you all right?"

Clarissa! This was Old Man Crampton, Theo realized. She was standing in the middle of the Jasper, Texas, junkyard!

Old Man Crampton stared at Theo. "My, my," he said softly. "No one's been near here since I moved in six months ago."

"I was just exploring, sir," Theo said. "I found this pile of— We were just having fun."

"I see," said Old Man Crampton. "Well, go on and enjoy yourself. By the way, what's your name?"

"Theo, sir."

"Well, mine's not sir. It's Otis." He smiled.

Theo was shocked. Was this the man who swallowed kids whole? She summoned her courage and asked, "Why do you live here?"

Otis pointed to the pile of junk. "Because these are the tools of my trade." He winked and walked away.

Theo set to work. She made a chariot for Clarissa
and placed a crown on her head. For herself she found
a helmet and a magic cape.

Most of the afternoon had passed when Theo waved
good-bye to Otis and Clarissa.

When she got to town, Theo stopped at the bakery
to tell Miss Betty Anne about Otis. But no sooner had
she opened the door than Miss Betty Anne cried,
"What a sight you are! Don't even think about coming
in here! Why, you'll scare all my customers away!"

Mudd Doogan received Theo the same way. "Get on home and fix yourself up. That's no way for a young lady to dress!"

Fortunately, Aunt Mazel was there. She studied Theo for a moment, then said, "I think it's quite clever, really. Why should a saucepan have one purpose only?"

Back at home, Aunt Mazel listened while Theo told her about the enchanted kingdom she'd discovered and the friends she'd made. "Well," said Aunt Mazel, "maybe people *would* like Otis Crampton. But I doubt they'll get close enough to find out."

Early the next morning, Theo returned to the junkyard. Otis was nowhere to be found. She walked
through his open front door and made her way to a
room where Otis was busy drawing.

"Theo! Come tell me what you think."

"I love it! What is it?"

"An idea I've been working on for a sculpture. I'm
going to build it right away—for you."

"Oh, my!" Theo said. And at that moment she
realized this was her chance to prove the town wrong.

After a couple of weeks of hard work, the sculpture
was finished. It was time for Theo to make her move.
With Otis's permission, she took Clarissa for a stroll
through town.

Just as Theo had expected, it was love at first sight
for the kids.

They all followed Clarissa home.

Music and laughter from the junkyard were heard
across the town. "What's going on over there?" cried
Mayor Mosely. "We must put a stop to it, whatever
it is." Everyone agreed.

When the people of Jasper, Texas, reached the
top of the north hill, they witnessed something
extraordinary below! The old junkyard had become
a work of art! A world of magic and wonder!

Following Aunt Mazel, everyone went down to get a closer look—not only at the junkyard but, finally, at their new neighbor, Otis Crampton. Theo beamed at the crowd—and waved at Mrs. Percy.